SkippyjonJones
AND THE
BIG
BONES

SCHOLASTIC INC.
New York Toronto London Auckland Sydney
Mexico City New Delhi Hong Kong Buenos Aires

JUDY SCHACHNER

For all those good people who keep my head screwed on tight—
Lucia, Heather, Sara, Steph, Margaret, and Rosanne.
And for Señor Meltzer, a real Menschito.

Love,
Judy

ISBN-13: 978-0-545-11406-6
ISBN-10: 0-545-11406-3

12 11 10 9 8 7 6 5 4 3 2 1   8 9 10 11 12 13/0

Printed in the U.S.A.   08

First Scholastic printing, October 2008

Designed by Heather Wood

The illustrations for this book were created in acrylics and pen and ink on Aquarelle Arches watercolor paper.

Skippyjon Jones was crazy about digging
in Mrs. Dolly Doohiggy's garden.

Because that's where Mrs. Dolly
Doohiggy's dog, Darwin, buried all of
his bones.

And nobody messed with Darwin.

Two yards away, Mama Junebug Jones was hanging wash when her kitty boy blew through the sheets like a muddy wind.

"Hey, Pickle Pants!" hollered Mama. "Don't run with your mouth full."

But Pickle Pants had only one thing on his mind . . .

. . . dinosaurs.

"I'm going to be a famous paleontologist!" whispered Skippyjon Jones, arriving at his room.

Then he popped a pickle in his puss. He slapped some glue all over his newfound bone and stuck it onto his model.

"And you are my Skipposaurus!" he added out loud.

"Skipposaurus!" declared Mama Junebug Jones, coming into the room.

"Those bones belong to **Darwin**, and you better take them **back**, for your prehistoric **fossil** is that snoozing doggy's **snack!**

"And do it now," ordered Mama, "before he wakes up."

But the kitty boy had no intention
of returning Darwin's bones before
he bounced on his big-boy bed.

First he

pounced

and wiggled.

Then he

bounced

and giggled.

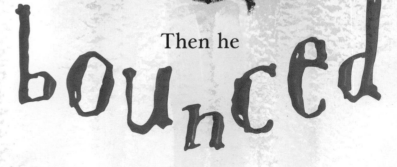

All the way up to the ceiling,
he chanted:

"Oh, I'm Skippyjon Jones,

And I bounce on my bed,

Cuz I love to eat pickles

That tickle my head."

Then he flung himself over to the mirror for a head check.

"Holy Hairballs!" exclaimed Skippyjon Jones, pulling out his tape measure. "That's one huge **cabeza!**"

Then, using his very best Spanish accent, he added, "My ears are too beeg for my head, and my head won't fit into my bed. I know I'm not a *Siamese cat* . . . I am a **Chihuahua!**"

And quicker than you can say "chunky Chihuahuas 'n cream," the kitty boy picked up his cape and pulled on his mask. Then he began to sing in a *muy* soft voice:

"Oh, my name is Skippito Friskito, (clap-clap)

And I hunt for the dinosaur-ito (clap-clap)

With gigantico ears

That's been buried for years

Under layers of sediment-ito." (clap-clap)

At the same time, the kitty boy's sisters, Ju-Ju Bee, Jezebel, and Jilly Boo Jones, were in Mrs. Doohiggy's yard watching Darwin sleep.

"This is fun," said Jezebel.
"Lotsa fun," agreed Jilly Boo.
"The mostest fun," added Ju-Ju Bee.

But Skippyjon wasn't thinking Darwin. He was thinking dinosaurs. And he knew where to find them: deep within his closet.

"Whoa!" said Skippito. "It's a jungle in here."

But as soon as he stepped over the threshold, his snifferito picked up the scent of his old *amigos*, Los Chimichangos.

"Stinkitos!" called out Skippyjon Jones. "I smell you but I don't see you. It is I, El Skippito Friskito, the great sword fighter."

"Up here, Skippito," hollered the Chihuahuas. "We are toasting *los marshmallocitos prehistóricos.*"

"Not the prehistoric

MARSHmallows!"

exclaimed Skippito.

"*Sí*, dude," replied the doggies, "but they are as hard as *rocas*."

"That's because they are fossilitos," said Skippito.

"Fossilitos, schmossilitos," declared Poquito Tito, the smallest of the small ones. "We want to see *los dinosaurios* with our own *ojos*," he said, pointing to his eyes.

"*¿Por qué?*" asked Skippito.

"Because, Bobocito," said Don Diego, the biggest of the small ones, "we hear they are reelly, reelly beeg, dude!"

This news made the Chihuahuas go insane-o
around the rim of the volcano, singing:

"Ding-a-ling, ding-a-long, ding-a-lito,

You are such a silly Skippito.   (clap-clap)

(clap-clap)

You know what dogs think:

If it's good it must stink!

Plus it's great for the old snifferito!"

(clap-clap)

But right in the middle of their romp,
Mount Itchee Gitchee Gumba blew its top,
tossing the doggies right on their rumpitos.

But a bump on the rump would
become the least of their worries . . .

. . . because **BOOM BOOM**

(BOOM BOOM)

boom *boom*...

the earth began to tremble and shake.

"*¡Terremoto!*" shouted
Poquito Tito, panic-stricken.
"It's not an earthquake-ito," said
Skippito, peeking through the bushes.
"It's a T. Mexito!"

And he wasn't the only *dinosaurio*.

There were big ones
and small ones,

feathered and bald ones.

Some were spiky and frilled
(with a look that could kill).

And they were all doing
the very same thing:
they were dancing.

**"¡Ay, _Caramba!_
It's the _rumba!_"**
cheered the Chimichangos.

And before Skippito could warn
them, the rascalitos had shimmied
and shook their way into the dance
line.

"This is loco!" wailed Skippito.
"You will be crushed like crispitos beneath
the dinos' toes-titos!"

But the pupitos did not hear.
They were too busy singing:

"Itchee Gitchee Gumba!

Dinos do the rumba

With jumbo jaws

And giant claws,

With horns and beaks

And scaly peaks.

Itchee Gitchee Gumba!

Chimichangos do the rumba

With great big hearts

And tiny parts,

With knobby knees

And lots of fleas.

Itchee Gitchee Gumba!"

But something had to be done to save them.
And quicker than you can say *Pachycephalosaurus*,
Skippito let out a . . .

big Jurassic-o
bark!

RRRRRRRRRRRRuffffffff!

"Holy Halitosis!" roared the T. Mexito. "I smell the pickle breath of a Skipposaurusito!"

"I am **not** a Skipposaurus!" declared Skippito, whipping off his mask. "I'm a
Chihuahua!"

"Not the
pillow-fighting, *ankle*-biting,
pickle-dripping, *dino*-tripping
Chihuahua they call El Skippito Friskito, the
Great Sword Fighter?" shrieked the T. Mexito.

"Oh, *sí*, that is me,"
said Skippito with a bow.

Then, quicker than you can say "Don Diego's Dominos," every *dinosaurio*

stopped,
dropped, &
rolled
far away.

"Where's the *fuego*, dudes?" asked Poquito Tito.

"There's no fire," said Skippito.

"They're just going extincto."

"*Muy bueno*, Skippito! We love the stinkito!"
agreed the Chihuahuas. And they tossed him
into the air.

"Diggeree diggeroo diggerito! (clap-clap)

We learned something new from Skippito! (clap-clap)

He scares them to death

With his old pickle breath,

And that's how
we get fossilitos!" (clap-clap)

Then, all of a sudden,

BOOM BOOM

(BOOM BOOM)

boom

boom.

The earth began to tremble and shake.
Every head popped up and sniffed.

"*Dinosaurios*," whispered the *perritos*.
"No," said Skippito. "They are extincto."
"*Sí*," said the Chihuahuas. "Es *muy* stinkito."

But it wasn't the *dinosaurios*
that smelled . . .

. . . it was **Darwin,** and he was
knock
knock
knockin'
on Skippy's closet door.

Then, *click*. The door opened and out tumbled the kitty boy on an avalanche of old dog bones.

The next thing he knew, the kitty boy
was waking up on the couch.
"What happened?" asked Skippyjon.
"Don't you remember, Sugar Beet?" asked
Mama Junebug Jones. "You decided to
return Darwin's dog bones."

"All of them?" asked Skippy.
"That's right, dumplin'," said Mama, proudly.

That very same night, the kitty boy
found Mr. Purrfect still sitting in the
corner all covered in bones.
  "My Skipposaurus," he whispered.
Then he dragged the cat over to his
big-boy bed for a good-night bounce.

"Oh, I'm Skippyjonjones,
  And I'm not a dog fighter,
  But I still have some bones
  'Cuz I'm the decider."

Then he decided to go to sleep.